A SECOND HANDBOOK

OF ETIQUETTE

FOR YOUNG LADIES

AND GENTLEMEN

TO BE USED AS A GUIDE

FOR EVERYDAY

SOCIAL BEHAVIOR

WHAT DO YOU DO

DEAR?

ʏ *Sesyle Joslin*

ɪᴄᴛᴜʀᴇꜱ ʙʏ *Maurice Sendak*

IarperCollins Publishers

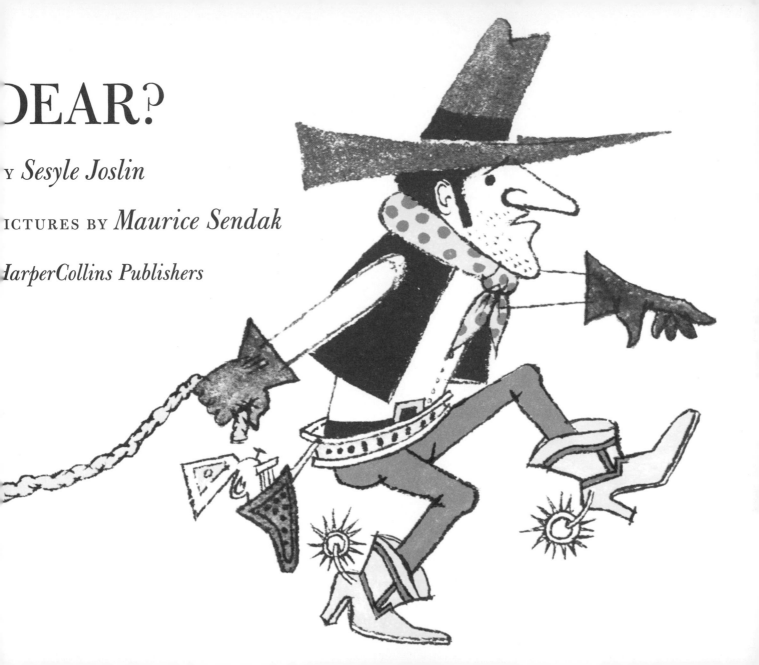

You are in the library reading a book when suddenly you are lassoed by Bad-Nose Bill. "I've got you," he says, "and I'm taking you to my ranch, pronto. Now get moving."

What do you do, dear?

Walk through the library quietly.

You have gone to a tropical island with your friend, the Pirate, to help him find buried treasure. You spend the entire morning digging for it, but then — just as you uncover a large treasure chest — the Pirate's cook rings a bell. "Luncheon is now being served," he says.

What do you do, dear?

Wash your hands before eating.

You are an Indian chief and you invite some cowboys to sit around the fire and smoke the peace pipe. But when it is your turn to puff on the pipe, you accidentally swallow quite a lot of smoke.

What do you do, dear?

Cover your mouth when you cough.

You are one of Robin Hood's merry men and you are sitting in Sherwood Forest reading a good book. Suddenly the Sheriff of Nottingham appears and he says, "I must take you to jail although, forsooth, I am sorry to interrupt you while you are reading."

What do you do, dear?

Find a bookmark to save your place.

You are a brave knight and you are sitting at the round table with nothing to do because it is raining. Suddenly the Princess calls you up. "Prithee, come rescue me," she says. "It is raining so hard that my castle is floating away."

What do you do, dear?

Put on your rubbers

before you go out in the rain.

You are at the North Pole, sitting in your igloo eating a bit of blubber, when in comes a huge lady polar bear wearing a white fur coat.

What do you do, dear?

Help her off with her coat.

You are riding downtown in a rather crowded howdah. The elephant stops at the corner and a lady climbs aboard, but there is no place for her to sit.

What do you do, dear?

Offer your seat to the lady.

You are a terrible pirate making a fine lady walk the plank, but when the lady turns to wave farewell to you, she drops her handkerchief.

What do you do, dear?

Pick up the handkerchief and return it to the lady.

You have just taken a great mouthful of pudding when into the dining room rides a handsome prince on a white horse. He says, "I am a handsome prince. Would you care to marry me?"

What do you do, dear?

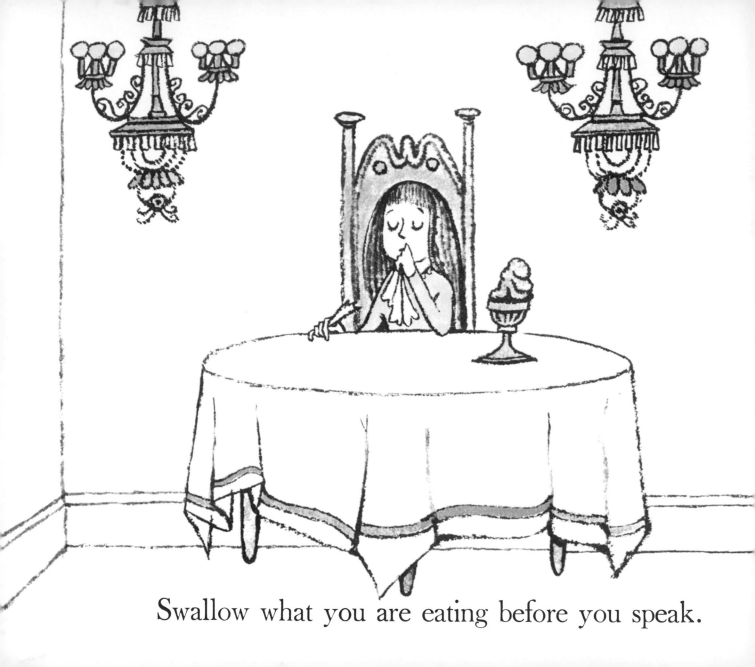

Swallow what you are eating before you speak.

You are a circus acrobat walking on the high tightwire and you happen to meet a lady tightrope walker coming from the opposite direction.

What do you do, dear?

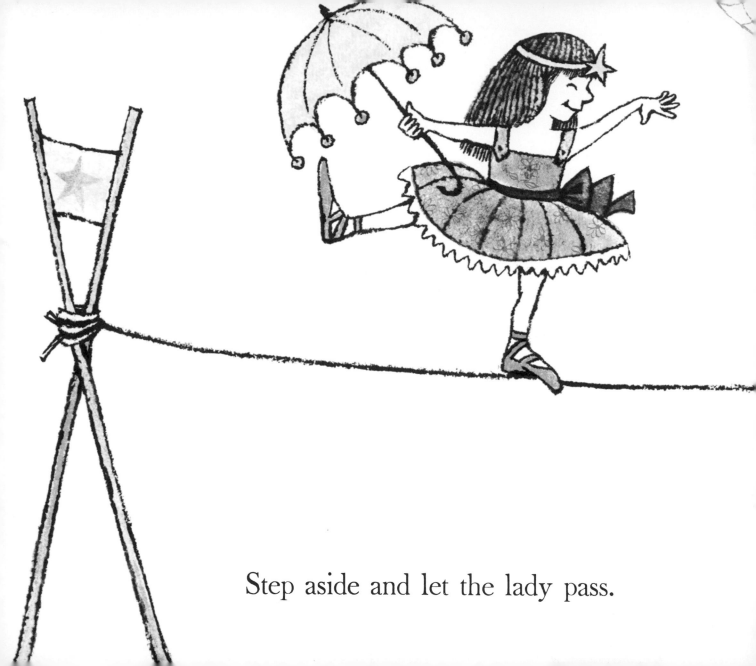

Step aside and let the lady pass.

You and your friends are at the Princess'
birthday party and everybody is having a
delightful time, only then the footman
announces the unexpected arrival of a large
and hungry dragon.

What do you do, dear?